RAISING THE STEAKS

IRON & FLAME COZY MYSTERIES, BOOK 1

PATTI BENNING

SUMMER PRESCOTT BOOKS PUBLISHING

Copyright 2024 Summer Prescott Books

All Rights Reserved. No part of this publication nor any of the information herein may be quoted from, nor reproduced, in any form, including but not limited to: printing, scanning, photocopying, or any other printed, digital, or audio formats, without prior express written consent of the copyright holder.

**This book is a work of fiction. Any similarities to persons, living or dead, places of business, or situations past or present, is completely unintentional.

ONE

The sound of clinking dishes and chatter from the kitchen filled the air. Lydia Thackery ignored it all, standing with her back to the wall on the other side of the swinging doors that separated her domain from that of the waitstaff. She was gazing out across Iron and Flame's dining room. Not *glaring*—just looking. Her ex-husband, Jeremy Montrose, was the focus of this look. Or rather, his newest paramour was.

Audrey Morrice deserved all of the unprofessional glares in the world. Lydia was having a difficult time keeping her expression neutral. She didn't care if Jeremy dated, really. Their divorce had been as amicable as possible. She wasn't still in love with him, and there was about as much chance of her winning the lottery as there was of her getting back together with him. Since she didn't buy lottery tickets, that chance was pretty much zero.

But *Audrey*. If there was one person who she dearly wished she had a good reason to ban from her restaurant, it was Audrey.

"Can you believe she keeps coming back?"

She turned her head slightly to glance at the asker of the question out of the corner of her eye. Brian Joseph was one of her sous-chefs, and in this case, apparently, her co-commiserater.

"Don't you have work to do?" she asked.

Her tone was tired. There was nothing sharp in the question, and Brian didn't even blink, for all that she was his boss. Well, one of his bosses. They were currently spying on his other boss. For all that they had managed to work things out so far, Lydia very much did not recommend trying to run a restaurant with one's ex-husband.

"It's my break," Brian said, lifting his half-empty glass of water as if in proof. "I have four minutes left."

She sighed. The fact that all of the kitchen staff got regular breaks even on the most hectic days was a point of pride for her. She had done her time in other restaurants, and she knew how bad it could get without good management, but though she would never say it, Brian was her least favorite of the staff. He always seemed to find ways to hang around her when they were working together, and was so hyper aware of what she was doing that she sometimes tripped over him when she turned around to grab a pan or mixing bowl off the counter, only to find that he was already handing it out to her.

It was nothing overt. Nothing that she could fire him for or even use as an excuse to bring the issue up to him without appearing completely arrogant, but she knew she wasn't imagining the way he watched her whenever they were in the kitchen together. She was thirty-two to his twenty-four, and more than that, she was his boss. Even if she wanted to start parading a train of dating partners in front of her ex-husband's face like he did to her, Brian certainly wouldn't make her list of choices.

It was strange. Before she and Jeremy had come to the decision to divorce, working at the restaurant had been her escape. She had felt more comfortable here than anywhere else, including at home with her husband. Now, more and more, she found that coming into work was a stressful experience, and her tense shoulders only relaxed when she stepped through the door of her rented house. Her home might be quiet and empty, but sometimes that was better than being surrounded by people who only made her feel lonelier.

"I can't believe they got back together," Brian added when she didn't respond. He was talking as if they were a pair of friends out to lunch, not two professionals on the job. "She spent the last month dating Hare Gill, you know. They even came here once. I think she timed it, so they would come in during one of Jeremy's shifts."

As much as she wanted to avoid gossiping with her employees, especially the one employee who seemed to want to view her as more than just his boss, that got her attention. Harold "Hare" Gill was a local who was known to have a temper. She couldn't imagine he was happy when the woman he was seeing went right back to Jeremy, and he was probably doubly unhappy if he realized Audrey had been flaunting their relationship in front of Jeremy on purpose.

"I didn't hear about that," she admitted. "What happened?"

"I've got no idea," Brian said, draining the rest of his water and leaning back against the wall as he crossed his arms. "But I saw Jeremy take her aside and chat with her while he was supposed to be in the kitchen cooking. *I* had to cover for him, of course. The next time she came in, about a week later, it was with him instead of Hare."

She had to grit her teeth to keep the words she wanted to say from coming out. As much as she hated how Jeremy used Iron and Flame as the main backdrop for all of his tumultuous relationships since their divorce, it would be completely inappropriate for her to say that to one of their employees. Despite their issues, Jeremy was still half owner of the restaurant, and they had only gotten this far because they had both kept to an agreement to make a show of supporting each other in everything surrounding their business.

"Well, my break is up," she said, even though it wasn't. "I've got to get back to work. Enjoy your last two minutes."

He pushed away from the wall and followed her into the kitchen, to her complete lack of surprise. "I might as well get back to work too. Hey, Chartreuse. You can take your break now, if you want."

Chartreuse was the other sous-chef working that evening. Unlike Brian, Lydia liked her. She was smart, quick on her feet, and was an excellent cook. Also, unlike Brian, she never tried to blur the lines between professional and not.

"Give me five minutes," she called back. "Got two more orders waiting for you guys."

Lydia looked over the order cards, feeling her stomach sour even though she had known what was coming. Audrey had ordered a porterhouse steak, cooked medium rare. She was proud of her cooking, and would never try to do less than her best, regardless of the customer, but she hated having to put her best foot forward for this woman.

She tried to forget who she was cooking for as she stood in front of the grill, letting the years of experience in the innate sense that had let her make a career out of her passion guide her as she prepared both the porterhouse for Audrey and the rib-eye Jeremy had ordered. She let them rest while Brian plated the side dishes, then watched as one of their servers, Noel, carried the plates out.

She felt a little more positive as she started preparing the next order. She didn't work the front of the house. She wouldn't have to interact with them. Within the hour, they would pay their bill and then—

"Chef Lydia, we need you out front." She paused, turning away from the grill to look at Noel, who gave her a sympathetic wince. "One of the guests has a complaint."

She didn't need to guess who the complaint came from. She handed the grill off to Chartreuse, then followed Noel out of the kitchen and over to Jeremy's table. It was a little gratifying to see that he looked embarrassed, though it was also a bad sign. Audrey, on the other hand, had no such compunctions.

"Oh, are you tonight's chef?" she asked, her voice dripping with fake sweetness as she looked up at Lydia. Lydia knew Audrey knew very well that Lydia was working tonight. They only had three chefs, and their third one was semiretired and only worked a few shifts a week. Still, this was a customer, and she could be professional even if Jeremy couldn't.

"Yes, I am. I was told there was a problem with your order?"

Behind her back, she made a subtle sign to Noel to let the girl know she could leave. She didn't want to make any of her employees deal with an unhappy guest if they didn't have to.

"Yes, well, I ordered the steak medium rare, and as you can see, it's completely overcooked. This is beyond well done."

She showed Lydia the steak that was cut in half on her plate. Lydia could see the interior, which was pink, right on the cooked side of rare. Even if she hadn't used a meat thermometer to ensure that this particular order was perfect, anyone who knew their way around a good steak would know Audrey was full of it.

But the woman was still smiling at her with that fake, sickening sweet politeness. Lydia glanced at Jeremy, half hoping he would chime in with his own expertise. He had been a chef for even longer than she had. But he wouldn't meet her eyes.

"I'm so sorry about that," Lydia gritted out. "Would you like me to take it back and make a new one for you?"

"Yes, please," Audrey said. "And do try to get it right this time. I'm sure you're busy, but I'd hate to leave a bad review for this place because you can't get it right."

Lydia snatched the plate off the table and turned away without another word. This was one of the reasons she hated Audrey so much. The woman did this all the time, unless she came in while Jeremy was the one cooking, in which case everything he made was perfect. She had no idea why the woman felt like she had to attack and belittle Lydia every time they came to eat at Iron and Flame, but there was nothing she could do about it. Not when making a scene would cause issues with Jeremy, and he had just as much power here as she did.

She was in a bad mood as she made a second steak for Audrey. Noel gave the returned steak a sad look, and Lydia pretended not to notice when it disappeared into a to-go box. They offered free meals to their employees once per shift—from a list, since some of what they served was quite expensive and they sometimes had a limited amount of it—but taking leftover food from a customer's plate was against their policies. In this case, the steak hadn't been touched except to cut it open, and even Lydia would have felt terrible just throwing it away. If Noel wanted to take it home, she wasn't about to stop her.

She was exhausted by the time the kitchen closed for the evening. The restaurant itself was still open for another hour as the diners finished their meals and the people sitting at the bar had their last drinks. She took a seat at the bar herself, not to drink but to unwind for a moment before she left for the night. Audrey and Jeremy didn't come in every day, but she never knew when she would see them or when Jeremy would be with one of the other woman he was dating. The not knowing added another layer of stress to her already stressful job.

"Oh, do you work here?"

The interested, excited voice belonged to a woman Lydia vaguely recognized. She was a regular, though not one who came in often enough for Lydia to know her name.

"Yes, I'm one of the head chefs," Lydia said, forcing a polite smile back onto her face. "I hope you had a lovely experience dining tonight."

"Oh, I just came in for a drink and a burger to go." She indicated the box in front of her. "I've been working all day, and I'm exhausted. You look pretty beat too."

"It's been a long night," Lydia admitted.

"You know, if you need help relaxing, I have something you might like." Lydia blinked and watched as the woman rifled through her purse, withdrawing two small vials. "These are essential oils. Lavender and chamomile. They're great for—"

"Sorry, I'm not interested," Lydia said, cutting her off. "And we have a no solicitation sign on our door."

"I just thought you looked like you could use the help," the woman said. "My name is Valerie. I can offer these to you for half off—"

"Please, ma'am, not tonight."

Valerie must have seen the look in her eyes, because she deflated and shoved the vials of oil back into her purse.

"Sorry." She sighed. "I know how obnoxious this is. I'm just really trying to offload all of these. I bought twenty cases of oil. A hundred vials per case. I thought it was going to be this great way to work from home, and everything else that woman pedaled to me, but now I'm out half my savings and no one wants to buy them. I'm at the end of my rope. I don't know what to do."

"I'm sorry," Lydia said. She meant it. She knew there were a lot of pyramid schemes going around, and she had empathy for the people who got caught in them. "You really can't try to sell them in here, though. I wish you luck."

"Thanks. They do smell pretty nice. At least my closet smells good now, even if I don't have any room to store my things with all the boxes."

Lydia chuckled, her first real laugh of the evening. "You know what, would you take five dollars for the lavender one? Nice smells never hurt."

Valerie gave her a crooked smile, and they made the trade. Oddly, after that interaction, Lydia felt a little bit better. She wished Valerie a good evening and left the restaurant, making her way through the parking lot to her little black SUV. She started it and then took her phone out of her purse, glancing through the notifications she had missed while she was working. The only one she felt the need to reply to was a text message from her sister, Lillian.

Are you free this weekend? Want to get together for lunch and go shopping? I feel like it's been forever since I've seen you.

Lydia thought for a moment. It *had* been a while since she had seen Lillian, not counting when her sister stopped in to grab food from Iron and Flame. But... Sunday was her only day off. And it was a day off from *work*, not a day off from *life*. She had a lot of stuff she had to get done, and she didn't think she would have time to spend a few hours with her sister.

Sorry, she replied. *I'm busy this weekend. Maybe next time.*

Only when she sent the message did she scroll up a little and realize that the message she had sent the previous week was almost identical, word for word.

She tossed her phone onto the passenger seat and backed out of the parking spot. Her life was a mess right now, but at least on the bright side, it could only go up from here.

TWO

There wasn't much Lydia was afraid of. Spiders she could do without, and the thought of losing the restaurant always filled her with dread, but overall, she thought she was a relatively confident, self-sufficient woman.

Waking up to hear her cellphone ringing in the early hours of the morning terrified her.

The feeling of dread that hit her when she came to was instant. Her first thought was of Lillian, and then of her parents. Had something happened? Has she been so absorbed in her work that she had missed her last chance to interact with one of her loved ones?

The number was local, but not one she had saved to her phone. She took a shaking breath and slid the button to answer the call, pressing it to her ear tightly.

"Hello?" Her voice came out as a ghastly croak. The response she got was not reassuring.

"Am I speaking with a Lydia Thackery?"

"Yes, this is she. How may help you?" Her words were automatic, giving away none of the panic she felt.

"This is Detective Bronner with the Quarry Creek PD. I'm calling to alert you of a possible homicide on a property you own in town—the restaurant, Iron and Flame. Are you able to open the building for us so we can retrieve security footage from your cameras?"

"I—yes, I can—a homicide? Are you saying someone was *murdered*?" Her voice climbed an octave as she spoke.

"Ma'am, we need you to open the restaurant so we can retrieve the security footage. I can get a warrant if I need to, but it will be faster if you—"

"No—no, I'm coming. I just—can you tell me who died?"

"Please just come to the restaurant, ma'am."

Frustrated, she jumped out of bed and rushed downstairs, slamming her feet into the first pair of shoes that she could find and grabbing her purse off of the hook near the door. She was still in her pajamas, but she didn't care. This felt like a bad dream. Someone had been murdered at the restaurant?

Her house was only a few blocks away from Iron and Flame, which was in an old, brick building downtown. It was one of the few standalone buildings in town, without any tenants overhead or other storefronts sharing a wall. It had its own parking lot, but when she arrived, it was cordoned off with crime scene tape.

She parked along the road and got out of her vehicle. A police officer intercepted her, but she introduced herself and said a Detective Bronner had called her. The officer led her over to a middle-aged man who was beginning to go bald. He had a lined face and a no-nonsense expression as he watched her unlock the restaurant. They didn't have a state-of-the-art security system by any means; just one camera at the front door, one overlooking the bar inside, and one at the back entrance. She told an officer where to find the machines the footage was stored on, but they wouldn't let her go into the building. Detective Bronner took her aside once she had done her part.

"What happened?" she asked as she looked around the parking lot, wide eyed. There were more police vehicles than she had ever seen in the little Wisconsin town of Quarry Creek, and the lot was lit with flashing red and blue lights. She saw a shrouded form lying on the asphalt near the middle of the parking lot, covered in a sheet. "Is that—"

"As I said, ma'am, this is a suspected homicide. Can you tell me if an Audrey Morrice is on your staff?"

"The security cameras won't have caught anything—" She broke off, blinking at him. "Did you say Audrey Morrice? Is that *her*?"

"Please answer the question, ma'am. Is Ms. Morrice on your staff? Would she have any reason to be here late at night?"

"No. She's a customer. She was here earlier, but she left hours ago. Is that ... is that her?"

"Please understand that we need to notify the victim's next of kin before confirming their identity. What is your relationship with Ms. Morrice?"

"She's dating my ex-husband," Lydia said. "I don't know her other than that. What *happened*?"

She thought of the woman giving her that fake, polite smile earlier this evening and felt sick. She didn't like Audrey, but she didn't think the woman deserved to *die*.

"Can you tell me if Ms. Morrice had any reason to be here so late at night?" the detective repeated.

"No," Lydia said. "No, she would have no reason to be here. We close at ten, and the bar closes by eleven. She left a while before that, though. You really can't tell me *anything*?"

"What is your relationship with your ex-husband?"

"What does that have to do with anything?"

He sighed, suddenly looking very tired, and she realized that he probably didn't usually work at three in the morning. She took a deep breath, trying to focus as he said, "Please, answer the question, ma'am."

"Our relationship is ... cordial, I guess," she told him. "We own the restaurant together. We divorced a few years ago, no cheating or anything major on either side. We just ... fell out of love with each other, I guess. I don't see what that has to do with anything, though."

"Will you be available tomorrow if we need you to come down to the station for further questioning?"

"Yeah," she said. "I don't have any—yeah, I will be."

He handed her a card. "My personal number is on the back. Please call the number on the front if you're looking for an update to the case. Be aware that we won't be able to share any information beyond what is available to the public. And please, give us time to speak to the victim's next of kin before you post anything about this online." His expression turned serious, and a little pleading. "No one wants to find out about their loved one's passing from a social media post."

"I won't post anything," she promised. "Am I ... free to go? What about the restaurant? Shouldn't I lock up?"

"You're welcome to wait in your vehicle until my men are done getting the security footage," he said. "Please do not cross the crime scene tape on your way back to your vehicle."

She swallowed and nodded, walking in a daze back toward her SUV. Her steps faltered when she saw a familiar vehicle pull up, parking a few spaces ahead of where she had parked.

Jeremy got out of it. He was wearing a faded T-shirt and old jeans, and she saw that he had somehow managed to mismatch his shoes. He must have gotten a similar call to the one she had received.

He paused when he saw her. "Lydia. Do you know what's going on?"

She opened her mouth, but no words came out. Her dismay at seeing him vanished in a flash when she realized what this would do to him. She didn't think Audrey was the great love of his life—she didn't think *she* was either, but she knew him well enough to know when he was serious about something, and Audrey had just been a way to pass the time for him.

But despite all of her internal conflict surrounding the man who was her ex-husband, despite all of the petty anger and resentment that had built up between them over the years, she knew he wasn't a monster. He wasn't heartless. He genuinely cared about his friends, and he had the potential for great kindness and empathy for all that, even though he had long since stopped going out of his way to show it to her.

Learning someone he was close to had died would crush him.

And Lydia… She didn't know if she had the strength to tell him. In the end, it was the fact that she didn't *know*, not for certain, that it was Audrey's body under the sheet in the parking lot, that decided her words for her.

"Go talk to Detective Bronner," she said tiredly. "I think we should close the restaurant at least through the weekend. I'll take care of it; you don't have to do anything."

She didn't know if he would be in any state of mind to talk to her after this, and she wanted to get that matter out of the way right now. If he disagreed, he could call her, but she didn't think he would. Closing the restaurant for a few days felt like the bare minimum of what they would have to do. She could already imagine how shocked and horrified their employees would be. They all needed some time to come to terms with what had happened, Jeremy most of all.

"Lydia, what—"

But before he could finish asking his question, one of the police officers approached, asking his name and what he was doing here, and Lydia hurried past him to her car. She rarely felt like she knew how to deal with Jeremy these days, and the horrible pity that was already welling in her as she watched through her car windows while Detective Bronner gave him the news just made things more confusing.

She hadn't liked her ex-husband for a long time, but maybe she didn't need to like someone to wish desperately that things could be better for them.

THREE

Lydia took a long bath when she realized lying in bed and chasing sleep wasn't going to get her anything but tangled sheets, and drank her coffee in the kitchen with the dawn.

It was a gray morning, overcast and cool, but the sound of birdsong filtered in through her cracked open windows and an adventurous squirrel was busy raiding the bird feeder in the yard across the street.

She watched the squirrel through the window beside her kitchen table as she sat there. She wasn't lost in thought—her mind was blank. There was too much to think of, but also not enough. Not enough answers for her questions, not enough information to even know which questions to ask.

Jeremy hadn't called her. She wasn't surprised but was a little relieved. Detective Bronner's card was sitting on her kitchen counter, but she doubted seven in the morning was an appropriate time to call the police station. She wanted, no, *needed* to know for sure who the victim was and what had happened to them.

Murder. Here in Quarry Creek, of all places. Tucked away in the wilds of northern Wisconsin, half an hour from Wausau, it was a cozy, comfortable town that had begun recovering from the loss of mining jobs and was well on its way to being a popular vacation destination for the people who lived in the more populated southeast area of the state.

It was not a dangerous town. It was not a town where murders happened.

When she realized her coffee had gotten cold, she drained the cup and rose to her feet to take it over to the sink. While she rinsed it, she glanced over at the clock on the wall next to the coat closet and started doing some mental math. She had the lunch shift today, which meant she needed to be at the restaurant from—

She blinked as she remembered the restaurant was closed. She couldn't remember the last time she had taken an unscheduled day off. It was Friday today, and the restaurant would be closed at least through the weekend, if not longer. She was glad she had told Jeremy she thought they should close, even though it had been a spur of the moment decision when she realized how hard this was going to hit everyone. She didn't even know if the police would *let* them reopen right away, and it would have felt obscene to have customers parking in the lot where a *murder* had taken place just the night before.

So, no work today. Or tomorrow, or the next day. She supposed she should try to talk to Jeremy on Sunday and reevaluate then. This morning, she needed to send an email out to all of their employees to let them know what had happened, so they didn't hear it secondhand first, and that they were going to be closed unexpectedly for the time being. After that ... her weekend was empty.

She set her coffee mug in the drying rack and stared down at her impeccably cleaned stainless steel sink.

She felt so *odd*; numb and tired and almost frighteningly blank. Was there something wrong with her?

With a deep breath, she braced her shoulders and walked through the doorway into the living room. Her laptop was set up on a little desk in the corner, beneath a framed photo of herself and her sister kayaking on the Wisconsin River. She and Jeremy had sold their house, splitting the proceeds during the divorce, and had both gone back to renting. Her landlord wouldn't let her paint, so the only decoration on her eggshell white walls were photographs and paintings, held up by sticky strips that claimed they wouldn't damage the walls when the time came to remove them.

The sight of her sister in the photo reminded her of the text she had sent Lillian the evening before. It felt like a terribly long time ago, for all that it had been less than twelve hours. Her sister had replied with a thumbs-up emoji and nothing else.

Lydia had felt bad for making yet another excuse not to see her, and now she realized her previous reasons no longer stood. She had at least three days stretching out in front of her with absolutely no commitments, and she was beginning to suspect that she needed someone to talk to, if only because picking every detail of the scene at the restaurant earlier that morning apart in her mind was going to drive her crazy.

Quickly, before pulling open her email program to start working on the notification to her employees, she sent a text message back to her sister.

Something came up, and I'm not working this weekend. If you still want to get together, I'd like to see you.

It was doubtful that Lillian would be awake yet, but as she turned her attention to writing the email to her employees, she felt better for having sent it.

Once the email was out of the way, and Lydia had showered and gotten dressed and had a second cup of coffee, she decided to get to work on some of the chores she was expecting to have to wait until Sunday to do. Grocery shopping was the first thing on her list—since she wasn't going in to work, she couldn't depend on the restaurant for one of her meals each day, and her fridge and freezer were getting worryingly empty. She usually meal prepped on her day off each week, but the two frozen containers of cabbage soup she had leftover weren't going to get her very far.

To get to the grocery store, she had to drive past the restaurant. The yellow crime scene tape was still up, fluttering in the breeze. It was the brightest thing she had seen so far on this gray morning, and the sight of it made last night seem all too real.

She drove past, hitting her blinker a few blocks down to turn into the grocery store's parking lot. She actually enjoyed shopping, usually, but she found that she could barely focus and had to keep glancing down at the list on her phone to remind herself of what she was getting as she pushed the cart through the aisles. Chicken, more curry paste, some coconut cream… She had written the list a few days ago and didn't know if she was feeling adventurous enough for curry anymore, but she didn't want to try to come up with a new list on the fly while she felt so odd.

"Oh! Lydia? I almost didn't see you."

Looking up from her phone, Lydia blinked, taking in the sight of the person whose cart had almost collided with hers.

"Melanie? What are you doing here?" Her words and tone sounded far too accusatory even to her own ears, and Melanie's eyes widened slightly in shock.

"Well, I'm grocery shopping," she said slowly, looking down at the eggs, pasta, and butter in her cart. She sounded puzzled, and a little hurt. Lydia winced.

"I'm sorry. I'm not myself today. I only got about three hours of sleep last night."

"It's all right," Melanie responded, giving her a kind smile. The expression turned into one of worry after a moment. "Did something happen at your restaurant? I saw the tape around the parking lot when I drove past this morning, and a friend of mine said she saw emergency vehicles there early this morning."

"Yeah. It was—" Lydia broke off, hesitating. What should she tell Melanie? She couldn't give Audrey's name, not yet —she still wasn't *sure* the victim was her, and she had promised the detective she would wait until they had a chance to notify her next of kin —but she thought everything else was probably public knowledge. "There was a murder there last night. A homicide. Someone was killed in the parking lot."

She realized she had just said the same thing three different ways, but Melanie didn't seem to notice. Her eyes widened.

"Oh, wow. Is Jeremy all right?"

Melanie Albright was a kind, wonderful woman who might have become one of Lydia's best friends in other circumstances. She also happened to be the first woman Jeremy had dated after their divorce, and the only one who had stayed in a relationship with him for longer than a few months. She had been half certain the two were going to settle down together, when they broke up out of the blue.

She *liked* Melanie, and she thought Jeremy had always been a little weirded out that his ex-wife and new girlfriend got along so well. She had always secretly hoped that wasn't the reason they hadn't stayed together. Melanie was *much* more welcome at her restaurant than someone like Audrey.

The thought put a sour taste in her mouth as she remembered that Audrey was most likely *dead*.

"He's fine," she said, but backtracked almost immediately. "Well, I think he's quite upset and shaken. I haven't heard from him since I saw him at the scene last night, but he isn't hurt."

"That's good, at least," Melanie said. "Can I ask … who was killed?"

"The police were vague," she told the other woman. "They had a name they were asking me questions about, but I'm not a hundred percent certain who the victim is, and I promised a detective I wouldn't spread the news today. They need time to contact the victim's next of kin first. I'm sure the news will leak in the next day or two."

"I completely understand," Melanie said as she placed a gentle hand on Lydia's arm. "I'll keep everyone involved in my thoughts. If you do see Jeremy, will you remind him that I'm here for him, if he needs someone to talk to?"

"I will," Lydia promised.

That was the other thing about Melanie. Lydia was almost certain that the woman was still in love with Jeremy all these years later, and she had no idea how to feel about it.

FOUR

An hour later, Lydia pulled into her driveway with a trunk full of groceries to find a dark blue sedan in her driveway and a detective waiting at her front door.

Detective Bronner turned around as she pulled up next to his car—she had a garage, but it was half full of boxes and furniture from her and Jeremy's old house, and the detective had parked on the wrong side for her to get into—and lifted a hand in a brief wave.

Lydia's heart began to pound as she shut her car off. What did he want? Why had he come here instead of calling her? Had something else happened?

She went around to the back of her SUV and popped the hatch, intending to grab the groceries, then wondered if she should have gone straight up to her front stoop to talk to him first. It would be even odder if she shut the back hatch before grabbing her grocery bags, so she gathered them up, feeling self-conscious the whole time.

Loaded down with grocery bags, she walked up the short concrete path leading from the driveway to the front door. Detective Bronner stepped politely aside as she dropped half of the grocery bags and fished her keys out of her purse.

"Good morning," he said. "I would like to talk to you about something, Ms. Thackery. May I come in?"

"Yeah," she said as she unlocked the door and picked her grocery bags up again. "Make yourself at home. Just let me put these down first."

She set the grocery bags on the counter while Detective Bronner stood in her kitchen, looking around. She vaguely remembered her reading some advice online suggesting that no one let the police into their homes unless they had a warrant, but she was too tired to care. She had nothing to hide, anyway. The worst thing he would find in her house was evidence of how utterly empty her life was, other than for the restaurant.

"This is about the murder, I take it?" she asked as she washed her hands. "Did you find out what happened yet?"

"The homicide is currently being investigated," he said. He was watching her closely. She focused on drying her hands off, and wondered if she was acting normally. She still felt so *numb*. "We have confirmed the identity of the victim and spoken to her next of kin, so I can confirm to you that the victim was Audrey Morris."

"That's horrible," she said, meaning it. "I saw her just yesterday." She closed her eyes. There was no way she could have known what fate awaited the woman, but she still felt guilty for her uncharitable thoughts the evening before.

"Ms. Thackery, could you please tell me how tall you are?"

She blinked her eyes open, giving him a blank look. "How tall I am? Why does that matter?"

"Please, answer the question."

"Five foot six," she said. "Without heels on."

"And do you normally wear heels?"

This was the most absurd conversation she'd ever had. "No. Never to work, and usually not on my days off either. Only on special occasions."

She was pretty sure the last time she had worn heels was the single date she had gone on a year after her and Jeremy's divorce. The date had been a failure, and she had tossed her heels in a closet and not taken them out since.

"I know we spoke briefly about your relationship with Ms. Morrice yesterday, but I would like to go into more depth today, if we can. Would you consider your relationship with her friendly? Did you see her or otherwise interact with her frequently?"

"We weren't friendly," she said, frowning. "She was … well, it sounds horrible to say considering what happened to her, but she was consistently rude and petty to me for no reason that *I* ever knew. I saw her a couple times a week at the restaurant while she and Jeremy were dating, and a few times around town other than that. I'm sorry, but I don't know how

I can possibly help you with this. We weren't friends, and I don't know much at all about her life."

He paused for a second before responding. He had a serious look in his eyes, and she felt her stomach drop. For the first time, she put all of this together and had to wonder ... was she a suspect?

"Can I see your hands please, Ms. Thackery?"

She knew by now that if she asked why, he would just repeat the question, so she held her hands out to him.

"Turn them over, please. I'd like to see your palms."

She did as he told her. He examined her hands, then gave a brief nod and she let them drop back to her sides.

"I have with me a warrant to look through your vehicle, Ms. Thackery." He withdrew a folded paper from his pocket. She stared at it.

"Why? I didn't do anything."

"Will you cooperate?"

"I'm not going to try to stop you, I just don't understand why you're doing this," she said.

He didn't respond, just stepped through the front door. She followed him until he told her to stop, then watched from a distance as he looked through her SUV, opening the glove box and feeling around under the seats. She kept her car clean, and he didn't find anything except for a few napkins she kept tucked away in case of emergency and a bottle of water that had rolled under the back seat at some point.

"Thank you for your cooperation," he said when he finished. "We may need you to come in for questioning at a later date, so if you receive any calls from the police station, please return them promptly. If you can think of anything you would like to tell us, please don't hesitate to call me."

With that, he nodded at her in farewell and got into his own vehicle. She stood by her front stoop watching, her arms crossed, as he pulled away.

The numbness from earlier was beginning to fade, and was replaced with a stinging feeling of unfairness.

Sure, she hadn't liked Audrey, and she hadn't made any secret of it, but she hadn't done anything *wrong*. She wasn't the one the police should be questioning.

She had to clench her teeth against a sudden wave of hurt as she wondered if Jeremy was the one who had pointed them toward her.

Turning on her heel, she went back inside. She wasn't sure that the stinging anger of being treated unfairly was any better than the morning's numbness, but at least it gave her energy as she put the groceries away and defrosted one of the frozen containers of cabbage soup for an early lunch.

As she waited for the soup to heat up, she checked her cell phone and saw that her sister had replied to her text message from earlier that morning. She also had a lot of other emails: responses from her employees to the email she had sent out that morning. She sat down at her kitchen table to read them, starting with her sister's message.

What happened? Is everything okay? I have to work today, but I could meet up anytime tomorrow or Sunday. Do you want to get breakfast together tomorrow morning?

All of a sudden, she could barely wait to see her sister. Lillian and a few of the friends who had stuck by her through the divorce were the only forms of social interaction she had, outside of work. Maybe she should make more of an effort to socialize, even though she rarely felt like she had the energy for it. She knew that her current lifestyle was unhealthy. Something needed to change.

I'm all right, and I'll tell you about it when I see you. Breakfast tomorrow sounds good. Do you want to come over or meet somewhere?

She sent the message and checked her other emails next. Most of the messages were short and simple, an acknowledgment that there would be no work this weekend and a few questions about what exactly had happened and if everyone was all right. Brian's email, though, was a little longer, and a little more involved.

I hope you're holding up. I'll keep my eyes open for another email specifying when the restaurant is reopening. In the meantime, if you need anyone to talk to or just want to get together for drinks, let me know. Funnily enough, my schedule just cleared up for the next few days. He ended the message with a smiley face. She stared at it for a moment, then closed her email program.

She would reply to the messages later. She didn't want to deal with Brian right now. She didn't really want to deal with *anything*.

With a sigh, she turned her head to look out the window just as a man walked by with a medium-sized yellow dog that had one ear that was pricked up while the other was flopped down. It was a cute mixed breed dog, and she felt a pang. She and Jeremy had been talking about getting a dog before he surprised her with the divorce papers. She didn't think it was fair to get a dog now, while she worked so much and lived alone, and she was allergic to cats, but she couldn't deny how nice it would be to have a furry companion to share her life with.

Yes, things needed to change. With the murder in the restaurant's parking lot, life was already changing, whether she wanted it to or not. Maybe she could take this unexpected time off to do some serious thinking and find small ways to improve her life.

She was only thirty-two. One failed marriage didn't mean her life was over. But no knight in shining armor was going to come rescue her from this tower of self-pity and depression she had trapped herself in. If she wanted to break free, she would have to do it herself.

FIVE

She spent the afternoon cooking. Some of her friends thought it was strange that her hobby was the same as her career, but to her, cooking for herself, in her own kitchen, couldn't have been more different than cooking in the restaurant for others. She loved her job, but there was always a certain level of stress to it. Everything had to be perfect, or as close to perfect as possible.

At home, she could relax and experiment to her heart's content. There was no one to complain if the food was too peppery, too salty or not salty enough, or somehow simultaneously both under and overcooked. She didn't have to worry about anything other than whether or not the food tasted good to her, and if it froze well.

She made a big pot of coconut chicken curry and another one of rice, then portioned the food out into separate glass freezer containers and let them cool while she washed the dishes. After the curry was put away into the freezer, she took the leftover rice, spread it on a pan, covered it, and put it in the fridge for her to make fried rice with tomorrow.

Since she didn't want to just live off of curry and rice for the week, she threw together a quick potato and cheese soup to join the curry in the freezer. It wasn't a huge variety of meals, but this way she could toss something home cooked and healthy in the microwave and have a good meal ready in minutes, no matter how tired she was.

Once she was done cooking and her kitchen was sparkling clean again, she changed into some stretchy pants and a T-shirt, tied her tennis shoes, and tried to psych herself up about getting some exercise.

Keeping a regular exercise schedule wasn't her strong suit, but she knew from long experience that working up a sweat would give her a much-needed mood boost. She still felt oddly fragile after the events this morning, and she was sure her lack of sleep wasn't helping, but it was too late in the day to take a nap and too early to go to bed. Going on a jog would at least help to relax her over-tired, over-anxious mind.

Setting out down the sidewalk at a brisk walk to warm up, she put one of her wireless earbuds in and hit play in the music app on her phone.

It felt surprisingly good to get out of the house and walk around her neighborhood. Quarry Creek was small, but not cloyingly so. It was well located, right off a state highway and close enough to larger towns and cities that they got plenty of day visitors. She had grown up here, until her parents moved for her father's new job when she was in high school. She hadn't ever been planning on moving back, but after going through school, getting experience as a chef, and deciding that she wanted to open her own restaurant, one of the only affordable listings for restaurant space she had seen was here. She had just married Jeremy, and he had thought it was a good idea—she was already familiar with the town and its people, and they might have better luck succeeding in the restaurant industry there than they would in a place that was completely new to both of them.

And now, here she was. Six years after opening Iron and Flame, and four years after her divorce. She *knew* she had a lot to be grateful for. Against all odds, her restaurant was a success. She had a few good friends, and her sister had ended up moving back to the area too, deciding she preferred small-town life.

Despite all of this, her life felt a lot emptier than she had expected it to be by her age. A few friends who she saw once a month if she was lucky, her sister, who she only saw more often because Lillian refused to let her stew in isolation for too long, and the restaurant she had devoted all of her energy to since it first opened. It was all more than some people had, but she wanted something ... more. As much as she loved being a chef, she wasn't planning on working until she was ninety years old and could barely lift a spoon. She wanted to work until she could afford a good retirement, and spend her elder years exploring new hobbies and enjoying the fruits of her labors.

She just didn't want to do all of that alone.

Sighing, she turned the music up and started to jog, wondering if she could make it through her usual route without gasping for air, since she had barely exercised during the past few weeks. Once she settled into her normal rhythm, it was easy enough to keep it up, and for a blissful few minutes, she didn't have to focus on anything except the sound of music in her ears and the feel of the pavement beneath her feet.

When she saw a man walking his dog down the sidewalk toward her, she slowed to a walk. The dog looked friendly, but she knew running past a strange dog obliviously was just asking for trouble.

Her steps slowed further as her lips tugged down in a frown. In fact, the dog and the man walking it looked familiar. Were they the same pair she had seen outside her window earlier? She was almost sure they were. The man had light brown, almost reddish hair and looked to be about her own age. His eyes were a lighter color, either gray or hazel. She couldn't tell from this distance. The dog was a medium-size mixed breed with yellow fur and one ear that was pricked up while the other was floppy.

It was a little odd to see them again, but it didn't raise any real red flags until the man's eyes met her own and he slowed to a stop, raising a hand in greeting. He said something, and she stopped moving, fumbling with one of her earbuds to take it out. She paused her music with her other hand.

"Sorry, what was that?"

"Oh, I didn't realize you were listening to music. Sorry to disturb you, but would you happen to be Lydia Thackery?"

She tensed and took half a step back reflexively. Mentally, she kicked herself for being so stupid. Another woman had been *murdered* not even twenty-four hours ago, and here she was, jogging alone, listening to music, and barely paying attention to her surroundings.

At least she was in her running shoes, and the man had stopped a few paces away from her. The dog looked up at her, its mouth half open in a canine grin as it wagged its tail, but she wasn't going to trust this stranger just because he had a cute dog.

"Why are you asking?"

It was a rude response, and she felt a little bad for it, but she thought it was fair considering the circumstances. A random man interrupting her jog to ask her name under normal circumstances was bad enough, but it was doubly alarming so soon after Audrey's murder.

"I'm Jude Holloway," the man said. "I'm a game warden, and I have an ID if you want to see it. I know this is unusual, but one of my former employees has been talking about you and some of the things he has been saying made me worried for your safety."

She blinked. A game warden? It was such a random profession that she almost had to believe it, but she was still weirded out by the whole situation.

"A former employee? Who? And how did you find me?" Her frown deepened. "Have you been walking around my block all day?"

His eyes widened. "No, not at all. I swear, I'm not a crazy stalker or anything. I walk Saffron a couple times a day anyway, so I just decided to come out here for her walks instead of going to our usual haunts, in hopes that I would see you."

"How did you know what I look like?"

He grimaced. "Pictures. The person I mentioned… He has a lot of them."

Her heart was still pounding. None of this was reassuring. It sounded like *someone* was stalking her, even if it wasn't Jude.

"Who is this previous employee of yours?"

"Brian Joseph," he said. "He worked for Fish and Wildlife up until about two years ago, and we stayed in touch after he left. It's only the past couple of months that I've begun to have concerns, but I kept contact with him to see if things escalated."

Brian? She had already been uncomfortable about some of his actions and the things he said, but suddenly all of his interactions with her came off in a new light, even the ones she had previously thought were innocent.

"And have they?" she asked, crossing her arms. "Escalated, I mean."

"I believe he has been stalking you," Jude said. He took his phone out of his pocket and swiped across the screen a few times before taking a step closer to her, holding the phone out. She took it cautiously and looked down at the screen as he continued,

"Unless you're aware that he has been taking pictures of you all over town."

What she saw on his screen made her stomach drop. Sure enough, there were photos of her—getting out of her car at the grocery store, coming into work, stepping out of her front door, even one of her driving, zoomed in through the windshield. For a second, she wondered if Jude had been the one to take these photos himself, but then she saw a picture that could only have been taken in Iron and Flame's kitchen, of her concentrating as she seared a steak.

Shaken, she handed the phone back to Jude. "How did you get all of these?"

"He's still friends with some of the younger guys at Fish and Wildlife," he told her. "He meets us at the bar sometimes after work. I overheard him talking to one of his friends about you, and it wasn't the first time. He left his phone behind when he went to grab more drinks, and I looked through it. When I saw these, I sent them to myself so I would have proof to show you. As for how I found you, he talks about you a *lot*. He mentioned what street you live on, and obviously, I knew what you looked like from the photos. I tried to find you online, but you don't seem to have much social media presence. I figured I'd run into you eventually if I started walking Saffron around here. I thought you would want to be made aware. From what I gathered, the two of you work together?"

She felt stunned—stunned and revolted. She had no idea someone was taking photos of her while she was out and about in her daily life. "I'm his boss," she said. "I'm part owner of Iron and Flame. He's a sous-chef there. I knew he was trying to push boundaries, but I thought I'd made it clear that I would never accept anything beyond a professional relationship from my employees. This is... I have no idea what to do."

"I'm sorry," he said, and seemed to mean it. His dog, Saffron, nudged her leg with her nose, tail still wagging wildly. "I know this must be surprising. If you need time to process it, I'm happy to give you my number. If you decide you want to press charges or pursue the matter somehow, just give me a call, and I'll help you gather whatever evidence you need."

"Thank you," she said. They exchanged information, and he wished her a good day. Whistling to his dog, who only left Lydia's side reluctantly, he headed the opposite direction down the sidewalk. She stood there for a second, watching him go, then felt suddenly too exposed out here on her own. She looked around, half wondering if she would see Brian's car somewhere, but the street was empty.

She wasted no time jogging back to her house and locking the door behind her. First Audrey's murder, and now this. She wasn't sure if she felt safe in Quarry Creek anymore.

SIX

By the next morning, Lydia had resolved to do everything she could to nip this matter with Brian in the bud. She was tempted to call Jude to see if he still meant what he had said about helping her, but she wanted to talk to Lillian first. Her sister would be horrified to learn that one of her sister's employees had been stalking her, but she would also have good advice. Lillian worked as a paralegal for a small, local law firm, and she had been amazingly helpful in finding Lydia a good lawyer for her divorce. If anyone knew what to do next in this situation, it would be her.

They met at a little café that was kitty-corner across the street from Iron and Flame. The crime scene tape was still up, and she wondered if the police would take it down, or if she was supposed to. She supposed she should probably ask them before she messed with it, but she had too much on her plate right now. She had no idea how she was going to manage to go back to work on Monday if she and Jeremy didn't agree to extend the time the restaurant was closed.

Lillian had the same red hair as she did, if a shade lighter, and had bright blue eyes without any of the crow's feet that had started to develop around Lydia's. Lydia was taller, but the two of them had been mistaken as twins in the past. Growing up, they had been almost as close as if they were.

Lillian was only two years younger than Lydia, but sometimes being around her sister made her feel ancient. The younger woman was bubbly, energetic, and never seemed to so much as take a day off.

They greeted each other with a tight hug before going into the café, which was named Morning Dove and had a stylized dove drinking a cup of coffee on its sign.

In addition to coffee, the café served sandwiches and salads. Lydia opted for a BLT, while Lillian got a scrambled egg and bacon breakfast burrito. They waited until they had the food in front of them before broaching serious subjects. The matter of Brian was forefront on Lydia's mind, but Lillian didn't know about it yet. What was on *her* mind was the murder.

"First, tell me how you're doing, honestly," her sister said, holding her gaze. "If you say, 'I'm fine,' I'm stealing your BLT and taking it home with me for lunch."

That surprised a snort of laughter out of Lydia. "I'm *not* doing fine," she admitted. "These past few days have been ... a lot. I think... I think I'm a suspect in Audrey's death."

The admission came out of her almost in a whisper. Her sister's eyes widened. "Tell me everything."

And she did, detailing how it felt to get the call in the middle of the night, to rush down to the restaurant and see the police vehicles gathered in the parking lot. She admitted how horrible she felt about her uncharitable thoughts toward Audrey earlier in the evening before she died, how badly she felt for Jeremy, and how frightening it was when she realized Detective Bronner was questioning her as a suspect, not just as the owner of the restaurant where the murder happened.

"I never wanted anything like this," she said fiercely. "I know I didn't like Audrey, and I never tried to hide that fact. She had earned my dislike, or I felt she did anyway. But I didn't want her to *die*, Lillian. I would never wish that, not unless the person was like a ... a serial killer, or something. Even then, I would probably feel bad about it."

"Hey," Lillian said soothingly. "I know. I believe you. Of course I do, you're my sister. I know you would never hurt anyone. Do you want me to help you find a lawyer?"

Lydia took a deep breath. "Not yet. If they bring me in for questioning, I'll call you before I say anything." The law firm Lillian worked for mostly handled civil matters, not criminal ones, but her sister would be in a better position to find a good criminal defense lawyer for her than she would be. "That's not my biggest concern right now, as strange as it sounds."

"Yes, that does sound very strange," her sister said slowly. "What could possibly be a bigger concern than you being involved in a homicide investigation?"

Lydia grimaced. For some reason, it was harder to tell Lillian about Brian than it had been to tell her about Audrey's murder, but she managed to get it all out.

Her sister frowned. "Do you trust this Jude guy?"

"I mean, I don't know him from Adam, but I can't find any holes in his story. One of the pictures he showed me had to have been taken in the kitchen at Iron and Flame, and I would definitely have noticed if there was someone who didn't belong in there. Considering everything else that has happened with Brian… I believe it. He sent me this email yesterday morning." She pulled up the email on her phone and showed it her sister. "He does a lot of things like this, and is always trying to get me to meet up with him outside of work. I've been trying to stay as professional as I can when I turn him down, and I act like I don't know what he wants. I thought that would be enough, but after seeing those pictures…"

"You're right to be taking this seriously," Lillian said. "What are your thoughts? What do you want to do?"

"Well, I definitely don't want him working at the restaurant anymore. I'm planning on contacting Jude after breakfast and seeing if he can help me get the evidence I need to file a police report, fire Brian, and also convince Jeremy that I haven't lost my mind. As much as I dislike working with Brian, he *is* one of our best sous-chefs. Losing him will be a blow, but I can't work with someone who has been stalking me."

"No, definitely not. If you need my help to find a good lawyer to consult, just let me know. I can ask my boss. Speaking of Jeremy, though, I got a weird call from him earlier this morning. I meant to bring it up to you first thing, but we got sidetracked."

"He called *you*? What did he want?"

"He was asking all sorts of weird questions about you. I thought he was just concerned, until I heard what you told me a few minutes ago. He asked if I had heard from you, if you had said anything about what happened, and if you ever said anything about Audrey."

"It almost sounds like he was trying to figure out if I'm the one who killed her," Lydia whispered. Her heart ached. Even with all of the issues she and

Jeremy had, she had thought he would know her better than that.

"You shouldn't care what he thinks," Lillian told her. She reached across the table, grabbing Lydia's hand and squeezing it tightly. "Of all people, his opinion should matter the least to you."

"But it does matter," Lydia replied. "If not to me, then it will to the detective who's working on the case. If they're looking for the killer, and my ex-husband and business partner tells them I had a motive to do it, why wouldn't they listen to him?"

SEVEN

They didn't have a game plan by the time they finished breakfast, but she still felt better for having talked to Lillian. Not for the first time, she was glad that Lillian had moved back to Quarry Creek too. They might not be as close as they had been when they were children, but she knew her sister would always be there for her in a pinch, and she would do the same for Lillian.

After breakfast, she sat in her car while she tried to plan the rest of her day. She couldn't do anything about Jeremy, Detective Bronner, or Audrey's death. That was all far, far out of her realm of expertise. She was a chef, not a hard baked private investigator or grizzled homicide detective. What she *could* do was try to fix this problem with Brian before it went any further. She hoped Jude Holloway was as willing to help as he had claimed the evening before. She didn't like having to rely on a stranger, but right now, she had no proof of anything Brian had done, besides a few too-familiar emails.

She had her head down and was on the verge of sending Jude a text message when someone knocked on the passenger side window. She looked up to see Valerie, the woman who had sold her a vial of essential oil at the restaurant on Thursday night, standing there. The woman waved at her, the smile on her face not fitting with how tired her eyes looked.

Lydia rolled down the window. She had absolutely no idea what Valerie might want.

"Good morning," Valerie said. "Sorry to bother you like this. I heard what happened at the restaurant; I bet it's been a crazy few days for you. I was just wondering, did you happen to try that lavender oil I sold you?"

"Not yet," Lydia said. It was sitting, forgotten, at the bottom of her purse.

Valerie's expression fell slightly. "Oh. I was wondering if you were interested in buying more. I'm trying to sell at least twenty today. I've got a bunch in my tote bag, if you want to see what scents you like."

Lydia stared at her for a second. On the one hand, she had never been a fan of anyone who was engaged in soliciting sales for anything. She had turned away more than one vacuum salesperson at her door. But on the other hand, she could imagine the stress Valerie must be feeling. Sure, buying the oils in the first place had been a bad decision, but now she was stuck with it. It sounded like she had spent a lot of money on them, and she had to be kicking herself constantly for having gotten into this mess.

"It is not something I'm interested in," she said at last. "I already have perfumes that I like, and I don't have an oil burner. I also don't wear any scents to work. Can't you return them? Or, didn't you say that a woman you know is the one who got you into the business? Can you talk to her about it?"

"They don't allow returns," Valerie said with a sigh. "And I can't talk to the woman who got me into all of this." She made a face. "Turns out, dead people don't exactly give refunds."

Lydia blinked. "Audrey's the one who sold them to you?"

"We go to the same gym," Valerie explained, leaning on the open car door with her forearms, to keep from hunching over awkwardly during the conversation. "She was really into this new company—she said she'd made a few thousand dollars selling their products already. It sounded like such a good idea at the time, and maybe she was just better at selling them than me, I don't know. I've barely been able to sell any, and I'm starting to freak out. And after what happened to her, I don't have anyone to turn to. The company isn't answering my emails, and I'm out of ideas. I don't know what to do."

"I'm sorry," Lydia said. She meant it, but, while it was uncharitable of her, her problems seemed so much larger than Valerie's. "Look, if you want to give me your number, I can ask my sister if she has any ideas. She works at a law firm. I don't know if she'll be able to help, but—"

"Oh, would you? Thank you so much," the other woman gushed. She reached out, and Lydia handed over her phone reflexively, watching while Valerie put her number into it. "You are a lifesaver."

"I'll give you a call if she has any advice," Lydia said. "I should get going, though."

"Of course. Sorry for bothering you. I'll hold off on trying to sell more of the oil until I hear back from you. I feel like an old-timey snake oil salesman." She wrinkled her nose. "It hasn't been fun."

Despite herself, Lydia chuckled and waved goodbye as she rolled up the window and pulled away from the curb.

She would text Lillian about the problem later. For now, she wanted to get home, and then contact Jude.

She sent a sour glare at the crime scene tape in front of the restaurant as she drove by, and planned out exactly what she wanted to text Jude when she got home. Or should she call him? It was a Saturday—she didn't know if he would be at work or not. He really had done her a huge favor by letting her know what Brian was doing. She didn't want to take up more of his time than she needed to. While he might have inadvertently added more troubles to her platter, she would rather know about her employee's stalking habits than not. At least it gave her something to focus on other than the murder. And now, she had a good reason to fire Brian. The thought of going into work and knowing for sure he wouldn't be there ever again lifted some of the weight off of her shoulders.

That weight came crashing right back down when she turned the corner onto her block and saw a very familiar car in her driveway. Jeremy was there, and he wasn't alone—a rusted old SUV was parked in the driveway behind his car, one that she didn't recognize.

For some reason, her ex-husband had made a house call … and he had brought reinforcements.

EIGHT

She pulled into her driveway, parking her car beside Jeremy's, and got out. Only then did she hear the shouting. And the pounding.

"What on earth is going on?" she snapped as she stepped between Jeremy's vehicle and the SUV and stomped toward the path that led to her front stoop.

When she saw a man pounding on her front door, she froze. He was a stranger, or almost a stranger. The burly, balding man who was currently trying to get into her house was Hare Gill, Audrey's ex, and the very man she and Brian had been gossiping about a couple of evenings before. He turned when he heard her and glowered at her.

"What are you doing here?"

His accusatory tone made her bristle. "This is my house. What are *you* doing here?"

"I'm trying to ring the skinny neck of the man who killed my Audrey," Hare retorted. "He's hiding in there, and he won't come out. Was he seeing you on the side? Are you in on this together?"

Hare thought Jeremy had killed Audrey? Jeremy was a lot of things, but he had never been violent, and she couldn't imagine where in the world this man had gotten that idea.

She also couldn't imagine what Jeremy was doing *inside of her house*. She knew she had locked the door when she left this morning, and he didn't have a key.

"I'm his ex-wife," she retorted, her voice sharp. "And I need you to leave. Right now. This is my property. If you have an issue with Jeremy, you can take it up with the police." He had a defiant expression on his face, so before he tried to strong-arm his way inside again, she slipped her phone out of her purse. "If you don't leave right now, I'm going to call 911. You're currently trying to break into my house. I have a security camera—I'll give them whatever footage they need to charge you with something."

The bit about the security camera was a bluff—she didn't have one, but she was certainly going to be *getting* one after all of this. The part about calling the police wasn't a bluff at all. Between the murder and Brian's stalking, she was at the end of her rope. She was done taking chances.

"Fine," Hare grunted. "I'm leaving. But you tell your ex, if I see him around town, he had better be prepared for a beating. Me and Audrey might have been on the outs, but I still loved her. She was my soulmate. He's not getting away with this."

She moved to the side, keeping space between them as he stalked back to his SUV. She made her way to the front stoop, but watched until he backed out of her driveway before she took her keys out of her purse and unlocked the front door, pushing it open to be confronted with Jeremy's terrified face.

"You made him leave?"

"Yes," she said. "And I'm about to do the same to you. What in the world are you doing here, Jeremy?"

"I needed to talk to you."

"What are you doing in my house? You don't have a key. And I have a phone, you could've just called me."

She pushed past him and shut the door behind herself while he scrambled to answer.

"You keep your spare key in the same place you kept it at our house, under that cat statue."

The cat statue was a joke gift her mother had bought her, calling it the closest thing Lydia would ever own to a real cat. It was made out of white stone with green eyes, and she had affectionately dubbed it Mr. Whiskers—not a name she would ever bestow on a real cat, but perfectly suitable for one made out of stone.

And yes, it had hidden her spare key for years.

"I can guarantee you it won't be there next time you go looking. And just knowing where the spare key is doesn't give you an excuse to go into my home. What gives, Jeremy? And what was with you calling my sister earlier? I met her for breakfast, and she told me all about it."

He winced. "I had to use the key. Hare was following me. You heard him, he's gone insane."

"So you led him here," she said dryly, tossing her purse onto the counter. "Thanks. I really appreciate it."

"Can you drop the attitude, Lydia?" he asked, seeming to have recovered slightly from his fear following Hare's near assault of him. "I really do need to talk to you."

"From what Lillian said, it sounds like you've been trying to figure out if I had motive to murder your girlfriend," she said, crossing her arms. All of her hurt was turning into anger. She was normally coldly polite to Jeremy, like she would be with a stranger she didn't particularly care for. It had been a long time since she had lost her temper at him.

"Well, I admit, I did wonder about it," he said. "Just think about how it looks. Everyone knew you didn't like her, and she wasn't exactly nice to you." He winced again. "I'm really sorry for that, by the way. I should have said something. That steak you served her was perfect, and the food was perfect all the other times she sent it back too. I don't have an excuse. It's just, I know how sensitive she was about us working together. It was hard for her, knowing that I saw my ex-wife almost every day."

Lydia sighed. "You're right, I didn't like her. She didn't have any right to act that way to me. She was rude and condescending and treated me like a piece of gum she couldn't scrape off her shoe. But you have to know I didn't do a thing to her."

"I do," Jeremy said. "After I got off the phone with Lillian, I realized how ridiculous I was being. I went to the sports bar, you know, the one that opens early —not to drink, just to grab a bite to eat and clear my head—and I saw Hare there. He didn't notice me at first, but it got me thinking... He's always been angry and violent, and he was extremely upset with Audrey when she and I started seeing each other. Out of everyone I can think of, he's the one who makes the most sense as a suspect. If he had asked her to meet up at the restaurant for a talk ... she would've done it, I'm sure. I don't think he would have planned it out, but if they argued and things got heated ... I can see him snapping and strangling her."

She frowned. "Strangling? Is that how she died?" she asked. He nodded. "How do you know?"

"Her mom called me last night. She was upset, as you can imagine, and let a few things slip. That's how it... Yeah." He looked dejected. "Someone strangled her."

She frowned, wondering if that was why Detective Bronner had been asking about her height. If there were marks on her body, the police might have been able to tell what angle the attack had come from, and whether the assailant was taller than her. Though why he had wanted to look through her SUV, she had no idea. Maybe it hadn't been done with hands? A rope, or a belt...

She shook her head, trying to dismiss the dark thoughts. "Well, I'm not saying you're wrong. I can see that. Hare certainly did look ready to murder someone just now. But you should have gone to the police about it, not confronted him."

"I didn't confront him. He saw me and started accusing me of all sorts of things. I threw down some cash on the table to pay my bill and left, but he followed me here. I wanted to talk to you, to apologize and to get your opinion ... and figure out what we should do about the restaurant."

"I don't think I'll be ready to reopen it on Monday," she said immediately. "I'm dealing with too much right now."

She hadn't told him about Brian yet. She still needed proof from Jude.

"Yeah, same for me," he said. "You want to wait until Friday? It means being closed almost a week, but we can take the hit, and I think it might be better to let things calm down a little anyway. Plus, that will give me time to go to her funeral without taking a day off."

She nodded. They *had* needed to talk about that, but she still wished he had just called her.

"You should go to the police," she said. "Tell them what you told me about Hare."

"I will," he said. "I was planning on going there after coming here. I really did just want to drop by, talk to you about the restaurant, and apologize. I figured Lillian might tell you about our conversation. I was… I've been a mess, Lydia. I can't believe she's really gone."

The grief in his eyes was enough to soften her anger. She heaved a heavy sigh and opened her freezer, pulling out one of the containers of the curry she had made the day before. She shoved it into his hands.

"Go to the police. Talk to them about Hare, then head home, eat a good meal, and get some sleep."

She didn't tell him to call her if he needed to talk. She wouldn't go that far, but she did know he must be suffering right now. She had stopped loving him a long time ago, and they weren't friends now. She didn't know if they ever would be. But she didn't hate him, either. As imperfect as he was, despite all his flaws, he was still the person who used to be her best friend.

That was worth some of her curry, at the very least.

NINE

After Jeremy left, she sent Jude a text message asking if he had time to meet her or if he would prefer that she call him. She was prepared to settle down with a cup of tea when he texted back, telling her he would be happy to meet at a local park.

She told him she would meet him there in twenty minutes, and made a list of the things that she wanted to ask him before she left. It was hard to refocus on the issue with Brian after her conversation with Jeremy. It was still pressing, urgent, and terrifying for her to think of, but the mystery around Audrey's death called to her.

Was Hare really the one who had killed her? She couldn't think of anyone else who might have done it, but Audrey probably had a whole circle of friends and acquaintances Lydia knew nothing about. There was Valerie, of course—being scammed into an essential oil pyramid scheme might count as a motive for murder—but when comparing Valerie, who was nice if a little pushy about selling her oils, to Hare, there was no comparison at all.

Only one of the two had threatened to kill someone in her earshot, and it wasn't Valerie.

The park was near the center of town and boasted a large water fountain that children liked to wade in during the summer months. Other than the fountain, there were walking paths, a few trees, benches, and a single pavilion with picnic tables and charcoal grills.

There were only a few people enjoying the park when she arrived. She spotted Jude almost immediately, mostly because of his dog, Saffron. She was on a long leash, and he was throwing a frisbee for her while he waited. Lydia approached him across the grass. When he saw her, he took the frisbee from his dog's mouth and waved at her. Smiling slightly, she waved back, pausing as Saffron trotted up to her and pawed at her leg, as if asking why Lydia wasn't petting her.

"Sorry," Jude said, pulling her back. "She's friendly, but I forget not everyone likes dogs."

"Oh, I do," she said, crouching to greet Saffron. The dog practically melted as she scratched behind her ears. "I just don't get a chance to interact with them much. Thanks for meeting me here."

She straightened up, and Jude gestured to a nearby bench. They walked over together, Saffron panting happily as she laid down at his feet. Lydia felt a little awkward, unsure how to broach the subject. Thankfully, Jude did it for her.

"So," he said, taking his phone out of his pocket. "I organized all of the photos. I also called him yesterday evening to chat, and recorded the conversation. I had to bring you up, but once I did, he started talking about you." He hesitated. "I think he's planning something. He said something about doing a favor for you, and being sure you wouldn't turn him down this time. I also reached out to a couple of the guys I work with, not friends of his, but coworkers who sometimes go out for drinks with the rest of us, and they agreed to give written statements about his behavior. I can email you everything right now. Do you think that will be enough?"

"I hope so," she said. "It will definitely be enough for me to fire him without any issues. I'll go to the police on Monday and see what they can do. Even just making a report will probably help, since that way they'll have it on record if he does try anything."

She gave him her email address, and he sent the files over to her. Once she confirmed she had received them, she relaxed a little.

"Seriously, thank you for this. I really appreciate it. I know you weren't obligated to do anything like this. You really went out of your way for me."

"Anyone would do it," he said. "Or, I hope they would. If you need anything else, don't hesitate to let me know. I actually went through a similar problem with an ex, who decided stalking me was the best way to try to get back together. I didn't end up taking it to the police, but sometimes I wish I would have. It was a very unsettling situation, and I don't think most people realize just how frightening it can be until it happens to them."

Oddly, she felt a little better knowing why, exactly, he had been so quick to help her. She wasn't normally a suspicious person, but after the murder and finding out one of her employees had been stalking her, she felt more wary than usual. But now that she knew he had experienced something similar, his eagerness to help made a lot more sense to her.

"This won't cause trouble for you, will it?" she asked. "I won't tell Brian where I got all of this, of course, but he might put it together."

Jude shrugged. "I don't work with him anymore, so I don't see how it could cause any issues for me. Don't worry about it." He reached down to pet Saffron, then rose to his feet. "I'll see you around. Good luck with everything."

"Thanks," she said, feeling like a broken record. "Swing by Iron and Flame sometime. I'll make sure you get a meal on the house—one of the benefits of being the owner."

He chuckled. "I'll take you up on that."

He waved as he walked away with his dog. She watched him go, hoping that one day she could find a partner like that. Maybe it was time to start dating again—once she didn't have so much on her plate, that was.

She opened the email again, this time intending to look through what he had sent her more thoroughly, but a call came up on the screen. The caller ID said it was Melanie Albright. They had exchanged numbers back when Melanie and Jeremy were dating, and Melanie had decided it would be better to befriend Lydia than stay at odds with her boyfriend's ex-wife. It wasn't the route most woman would have taken, but Lydia knew that their work arrangement meant that she and Jeremy maintained a very unusual relationship for exes, and anyone either of them dated would have to find a way to be okay with it.

And it had worked—she and Melanie had always been on friendly terms.

A little unsure as to what the woman might want, she answered the call with a curious, "Hello?"

"Hey, Lydia," Melanie said. Her voice sounded odd, more uncertain than usual. "I heard what you did. Do you have time to talk?"

TEN

Lydia felt as if her brain had short-circuited. Melanie had heard what she'd done? Lydia hadn't *done* anything, except meet with Jude, chat with her sister, and have a very strange interaction with Hare and Jeremy. Her mind immediately jumped to the conclusion that Melanie had somehow heard a rumor that she was the one who killed Audrey. Her mouth suddenly felt dry, and she found herself wishing she had brought a water bottle along to the park.

"What do you mean?"

Melanie laughed, a lighthearted sound that seemed at odds with her words. "Why, sending Jeremy home with some of your coconut curry, of course. It was so kind of you, and after how upset he's been, I know it means a lot. He called me, you know. He wanted to talk—to apologize. I ran into him in town yesterday, and he said something quite rude, but I know he was just upset. Still, your kindness seems to have made him feel better. I was wondering, what did the two of you talk about?"

Lydia felt like she had whiplash. She had absolutely no idea why this conversation was even happening. Why was she talking to her ex-husband's ex-girlfriend about how he was doing after his current girlfriend was murdered? How had this become her life?

"We didn't talk much." She paused, scrambling to try to remember what she and Jeremy had discussed. "He thinks Hare Gill is the one who killed her, but there's no proof. He apologized to me too, we chatted about the restaurant, and he left after that. That's about it. Why?"

"Oh, I just wanted to know what's going through his head," Melanie said. She sounded a little hesitant, that same odd note in her voice that Lydia had noticed when she first answered the call.

"I wasn't aware you still talked to him that much," Lydia said.

"We chat sometimes," Melanie said. "You and me... We're friends, right? I know it's a little odd, but I always thought you and I got along pretty well, and I completely understand how your and Jeremy's relationship works."

Do you? Lydia thought. *Because I don't, so please explain it to me.* But she didn't say that. Instead, she said, "I like to think we're friends too. I don't understand what this is about, though, Melanie."

"This is going to sound ghoulish, considering what just happened to Audrey, but I think we both knew they weren't serious. I've been wondering... do you think Jeremy's ready to settle down again? Once he heals from all of this, of course. It's that we're both single now, and the connection I felt with him is unlike anything I've ever felt with anyone else. You know him the best of anyone. Do you think he's ready for something serious?"

Lydia stared blankly across the park. Suddenly, she wished Jude hadn't left, if only because it would have given her an excuse to end this conversation early. "I really have no idea, Melanie. I'm sorry. I don't know what to tell you."

"I've been trying to move on," Melanie said. "But I can't. I don't know who else to talk to about it. I'll give him time, of course, but I really would like to try again with him."

These last three days had been the most insane of Lydia's life. This conversation with Melanie included.

"The two of you are going to have to figure that out yourselves. I'm sorry, but I've really got to go. I've got a lot to do right now, and some of it is time sensitive. Maybe we can chat later?"

She *did* like Melanie, but she didn't want to continue this conversation in the slightest.

"Oh, sorry. Of course. I'm sure you're busy. Just give it some thought, okay? I'm sure both of us would prefer he didn't start dating someone like Audrey again."

They said their goodbyes and Lydia ended the call, slipping her phone into her purse as she rose from her seat on the bench and started walking back through the park toward her car.

It was true that she didn't want Jeremy to start bringing another woman who acted like Audrey around the restaurant. Beyond that, she didn't care who he dated, but it seemed inevitable that his dating life would continue to affect her as long as they continued working at the same restaurant.

And neither of them were going to give up their claim on Iron and Flame.

If there was one thing she was certain she didn't want, it was to get involved in her ex-husband's dating life. She liked Melanie well enough, but the other woman would have to figure this out on her own.

As she reached for her car's door handle, her hand paused.

Melanie had what was beginning to seem like an unhealthy obsession with Jeremy. Melanie, who she had gone months without seeing or talking to, had suddenly reinserted herself into both Lydia's life and Jeremy's.

And all of it, only after Audrey had been murdered.

She didn't want to think it of the kind, empathetic woman, but the seeds of doubt had been planted.

Was Melanie the one who killed Audrey, all so she could have Jeremy to herself?

ELEVEN

Lydia spent that evening pouring over the evidence Jude had sent her of Brian's stalking of her. On Sunday, she took a much-needed day off. In retrospect, she probably could have gone to the police instead of waiting until Monday. She doubted they were closed on Sundays, but she had never actually needed to go to the police station before and had no idea what their hours were.

But she figured it could wait until Monday. She needed a day to herself. Sure, Friday and Saturday had technically been days off, but those were days off from cooking in her kitchen at Iron and Flame, not from dealing with the aftermath of a murder and a delusional employee. All told, it had ended up being a lot more stressful than her usual occupation.

She took a bubble bath, deep cleaned the house, made the fried rice she had nearly forgotten about, and sat outside in her little backyard drinking tea, trying to find the peace and serenity she had first felt back when she was house shopping and stepped into the backyard for the first time. It was one of the reasons she had rented this particular house instead of any of the others she had seen. The backyard might be small, but it had a wooden privacy fence around it, a lovely, old oak tree, and a little concrete patio encircled by bushes. It was peaceful, her little slice of nature and serenity away from the hustle and bustle of normal life.

She felt a little better by the time she went to bed that evening. Nothing had been resolved yet, but at least she had a plan to deal with Brian, and it seemed like she wasn't a major suspect in Audrey's murder anymore, if the absence of police swooping in to arrest her meant anything.

Besides, she decided when she woke up Monday morning, it was probably better that she talked to Jeremy about Brian first. He didn't like being stonewalled out of decisions that involved the restaurant. Neither did she, which was why she always made an effort to talk to him before doing anything out of the ordinary at Iron and Flame. Firing an employee for stalking her was certainly out of the ordinary.

She finished her morning coffee, made herself a bowl of oatmeal, and tidied up the dishes before calling her ex-husband.

"I was just about to call you," Jeremy said when he answered.

She rolled her eyes, not quite believing it. Jeremy was always just about to do something, but never seemed to actually do it until she made the effort first.

"Can we meet somewhere? I want to talk. It's about the restaurant."

"Yeah," he said, suddenly all business. "Do you want to meet there? I talked to that detective when I went by to tell them about Hare, and he said we have to take the crime scene tape down ourselves. We also need to take out the trash and get the spoilable food out of the fridge. We weren't prepared to be shut down for a week when you closed it Thursday night."

She winced. "Right. I completely forgot about that. Meet there in an hour?"

He confirmed, then ended the call. She got ready to go, putting on comfortable shoes, jeans, and a shirt she wouldn't mind getting dirty. She wanted to give the restaurant a good cleaning, ensuring it would be spic-and-span and ready to open on Friday. While she was glad they had decided to delay reopening the restaurant, a part of her was already itching to get back to work. It was familiar, and familiar was comforting.

Jeremy was already in the parking lot when she arrived. He had pulled down the crime scene tape and was bundling it into a trash bag when she opened her car door.

"It's good to see the parking lot looking normal again," she said.

"If I never see crime scene tape again in my life, it will be too soon," he agreed. "Let's deal with the trash first thing. The dumpster pickup is tomorrow morning, so we should get it all out today, so it isn't sitting out there for a week."

She hated throwing away food, but she knew he was right. Everything in the freezer and the dry goods in the pantry would keep, but a lot of their refrigerated items would be spoiled by Friday. Some of it had probably spoiled over the weekend. She and Jeremy both prided themselves on keeping a clean kitchen, and neither of them liked having spoiled food near the good food.

It was almost peaceful, working together to prepare the restaurant for another few days of closure. They were always at their best together when they were working toward a shared goal. Of course, it only lasted until Jeremy started talking.

"I've been thinking about what happened to Audrey," he said. She hadn't brought up Brian yet, or any other serious subject. She wanted to wait until they were almost ready to leave to bring it up, so she wouldn't have to spend the whole time they were there talking about it.

"Did you tell the police what you told me about Hare?" she asked.

He nodded. "They said they'll look into it. But... I'm beginning to think I was wrong. I think it might have been ... someone else."

She raised an eyebrow as she emptied the main garbage bin in the kitchen, tying the bag shut in a practiced motion. "You seemed convinced it was him. What made you change your mind?"

"A couple of things," Jeremy said. "First was the way he reacted to seeing me. Looking back at it, when I had a chance to calm down a little, I realized it seemed like he honestly believed I was the one who attacked her. Unless he's a better actor than I thought, it makes no sense that he would think I'm the one who did it if he's the guilty one."

She nodded slowly. Hare *had* seemed pretty convinced Jeremy was behind Audrey's death when he was trying to get into her house on Saturday. "Do you have any other suspects in mind?"

He hesitated. "Well, that's the thing. Melanie has been calling me more than usual over the weekend. We stayed in contact after we decided it wasn't the right time for us to date each other, but never anything like this. She's been great, of course, very supportive, but the timing of it seems weird, and I get the feeling she has almost been waiting for something like this to happen. I know it sounds insane, but... I almost have to wonder if she was involved, somehow."

Lydia might have laughed it off, if she hadn't had the same doubts about Melanie herself.

"Do you have any proof?" she asked. "Anything more than a gut feeling?"

He sighed. "No. I don't know, maybe I *am* insane. I mean, I suspected *you* at first, and obviously I wasn't right about that either. I don't trust my own instincts right now."

She frowned. She wasn't sure she trusted Jeremy's instincts either, but *someone* had killed Audrey, and chances were it was someone the woman had known. Hare and Melanie both fit that bill.

"Let me take this trash out," she said. "I'll be right back. I've been talking to her too, maybe between the two of us we can piece it all together."

She grabbed two of the largest garbage bags and headed toward the back door, pushing it open with her hip as she stepped outside. Making her way over to the dumpster, she dropped the garbage bags, then heaved the lid open. She tossed them in one at a time, and decided to leave the dumpster open, since they had more bags to bring out. They would just have to remember to close it when they were done—they didn't need a family of raccoons moving in. Again.

She turned to go back inside when a car parked across the street caught her eye.

She knew that car. She saw it almost every day when she went to work.

Brian's car.

A shadowy figure in the front seat leaned forward, and she felt a mixture of fear and anger rising in her chest. Had he followed her here, or had he been driving by when he saw her vehicle in the parking lot? What did he *want* with her?

As the driver's side door opened and he got out of the vehicle, she realized she was about to find out.

TWELVE

Lydia hesitated, wondering if she should go back inside and tell Jeremy that Brian was here, but she hadn't told him about the stalking, and it would all be a big mess. Still, she walked over to the door, keeping it at her back so if something happened, she would be prepared to duck inside.

"Hey," Brian called out as he crossed the street, his voice open and friendly. If she hadn't known the truth, she wouldn't have thought anything of him finding her here.

"Good morning," she said as he approached her. Her voice was too sharp, but he didn't seem to notice. "We aren't reopening until Friday, like I said in my last group email."

"Oh, I know," he said. "I just saw your car while I was driving past and thought I'd stop by and say hi."

"Well, Jeremy and I are busy cleaning out the kitchen. I should probably get back to it."

"Do you need help?" he asked.

She shook her head. "No, none of this is on the clock. You've got time off, why don't you go enjoy it?"

"I'd enjoy helping you out," he said. "Jeremy could go home. I'm sure he's still upset about what happened to that girlfriend of his. I'm happy to help you with whatever needs to be done."

She frowned. "No, we've got it covered. It was nice of you to stop by, but we really don't need your help."

She half turned, reaching for the doorknob, and he took a step forward.

"Why do you always do that?" he asked, beginning to sound upset. "I'm just trying to be helpful. I always try to go out of my way to do nice things for you, and it's like you don't even notice."

"I've never asked you to go out of your way to do anything," she said. "All you need to do is your job,

Brian, nothing more. I'm going to ask you to stop contacting me outside of work. I don't think it's appropriate."

Soon, he wouldn't have a chance to contact her at all, because she was going to fire him once she cleared the matter with her ex-husband. She didn't think it would be a good idea to mention that right now, though.

"Why can't you see it?" Brian asked, taking another step toward her. "I like you, Lydia. I want to be more than just employer and employee. Why don't you give me a chance? We could go out tonight—"

"No," she said forcefully. "I'm sorry to be so blunt, but I'm just not interested in you. You're my employee, so it would be completely against our policy, but even if it wasn't, you're eight years younger than me. We have nothing in common. Please, just drop it."

She inched back, and her hand closed around the door handle, but Brian wasn't taking the hint. He strode forward, grabbing her wrist before she could open the door.

"Why do you have to be so difficult?" he snapped. "I've been trying to get you to notice me ever since I started working here. Can't you see that you mean more to me than just being my employer? I've done so much for you, more than you know about. Just give me one chance. Unlike your ex-husband, I'm not going to stand by and let someone else insult your cooking, or anything about you. I'll take care of it, and make sure they never bother you again."

He was staring at her intensely, and Lydia felt something cold slip into her veins.

"What ... what do you mean?" she asked. "What have you done for me that I don't know about?"

He paused, searching her face as if looking for something. She had no idea what he saw in her expression, but he gave a tight nod, though he didn't release her wrist.

"Well, Audrey isn't going to bother you anymore, is she?" he asked, his voice low. "I've seen her come in, week after week, berating you when you did nothing wrong. I couldn't stand it anymore. You didn't deserve that."

"Did you kill her?" The words came out in a whisper.

"I did it for you," he said, his voice filled with feeling. "It was easy enough to get her out here. I used the restaurant's email and pretended to be you. I told her you needed to tell her something important about Jeremy. I hid around the corner. She didn't get a chance to see me coming up behind her. I had no idea it would take so long to strangle someone, but I'm still glad I did it. She won't ever bother you again. You're free. And I won't let anyone else bother you either. You just need to give me a chance."

She took a deep breath to scream, but her throat didn't seem to be working. Her thoughts felt like they were spinning around in circles.

Brian was the killer. She and Jeremy had both been barking up the wrong trees this entire time. This had nothing to do with him or Audrey, not really. It was all about *her*, in the worst possible way.

And now, here she was, trapped behind her restaurant with Audrey's killer holding onto her wrist.

Thinking quickly, she slammed the heel of her shoe back into the door, hoping the loud thud would draw Jeremy's attention. Brian's face twisted, and he yanked her away from the door, pulling her toward the street and his car.

"Why do you keep fighting this?" he asked. "We're meant to be together."

"Let go of me," she said, trying to pull out of his grip, but his fingers were like iron around her wrist.

The squeal of brakes made her flinch. The expected impact never came. The car stopped just feet away from her and Brian, who swore at the driver.

Lydia glanced through the windshield and felt her spirits lift when she saw who was on the other side. Jude. He opened the car door and stepped out, still in his work uniform.

"Let her go," he said, his tone far more authoritative than she had ever heard it.

Brian froze, and she could practically see his mind racing. Lydia didn't give him time to come up with a plan. She stomped down on his foot as hard as she could, and finally the grip on her wrist released. Yanking away from him, she scrambled around to the other side of Jude's car. Realizing that he wasn't going to get her back without a struggle, Brian began to back away.

"This isn't what it looks like, I swear," he said, giving a nervous laugh.

The familiar squeaking of the hinges on the restaurant's back door drew her eyes over to see Jeremy stepping out into the alley. He looked around, puzzled. When he saw her partway across the road, he called out, "Lydia? Where did you go? We're not done in here."

Brian turned and ran toward his car. Lydia took a step after him, wondering if they should stop him from getting away, but Jude stopped her with a worried look.

"We'll go in together and call the police," he said. "I'm glad I asked a couple of my friends to help me keep an eye on him. One of them said that he saw Brian's car parked across from your restaurant, and thought he was up to something. I was at work, but I managed to call out and came right over. I'm sure the police will be able to track him down even if he tries to flee. The important thing is that you're all right."

Jeremy was walking across the road toward them, his expression somewhere between annoyed and concerned. Lydia realized she was shaking. "I can't believe how stupid I was," she said. "He's the one who killed Audrey. And he did it for me."

"It will be all right," Jude promised her quietly, right before Jeremy started asking what in the world was going on.

EPILOGUE

It felt good to be back in Iron and Flame's kitchen, even though after Brian's arrest and Audrey's death, she didn't think anything would ever really be normal again. Thankfully, working in the kitchen meant that she could avoid the brunt of the public's curiosity. Chartreuse, who was working extra hours until they could find a sous-chef to replace Brian, was being extra nice to her, and Jeremy was mostly keeping to himself, though she had heard through the grapevine that he had gone out for coffee with Melanie a few times.

The two weeks following Audrey's murder had been full of slow healing for her. She felt as if she was seeing the world in a new light. Everything that happened had given her a new sense of appreciation for her sometimes quiet, sometimes stressful life.

"Ms. Thackery, one of the guests requested to see you, specifically," Noel said, poking her head into the kitchen.

For once, Lydia had no idea who it could be. Her mind flashed to Jude. She had kept in contact with him during the past two weeks, mostly keeping him updated on the charges Brian was facing, but she couldn't deny that she wanted to see more of him. A few text messages exchanged every couple of days somehow didn't feel like enough.

"I can be out in five minutes," she told Noel, who nodded and vanished back into the dining area.

She finished the next order's pan seared trout and left it for Chartreuse to plate before she stepped out of the kitchen. Noel walked past, carrying a tray full of plates, and nodded toward the bar.

Valerie turned and waved at her.

Lydia smiled, making her way over to take a seat next to the other woman. "I've only got a few minutes before I've got to get back to work. How are you doing?"

"Much better," Valerie said. "Thank you so much. I brought a gift for you." She stooped down and took a small gift bag out of her tote, handing it over to Lydia. "And thanks for your help."

Lydia peeked inside, and had to laugh. "I think I'm set on essential oils for life now."

Valerie grinned. "Well, the idea to start selling them online helped a lot. I made up another gift bag for your sister. But really, Lydia, thank you. I was at the end of my rope, and without you, I don't know what I would've done."

Lydia smiled back at her. True to her word, she had given Lillian a description of Valerie's problem. Lillian hadn't had any legal advice, but she had come up with the idea of Valerie opening an online store to sell the oils. It seemed to be working—Valerie was now slowly selling off her stock, and making back some of the money she had lost on the endeavor.

"Do you want to get together for drinks sometime? I don't know what your work schedule is like, but I'm always off by six, so my evenings are usually free."

"I work a mix of shifts, but I should be free tomorrow night," Lydia told her.

She had kept her word to herself, too. She had been making small changes in her life, which included making more time for her social life. Before, she would have made her excuses and spent the evening at home, trying to de-stress after a shift at the restaurant, and picking apart every small mistake she had made with the food. Not any longer.

"Tomorrow sounds great," Valerie said. "Invite whoever you like. We'll have a girls' night out."

Taking her gift bag with her, Lydia said goodbye to her new friend and returned to the kitchen. This was just the beginning, she promised herself. The beginning of living for herself, not for the restaurant or for anyone else. She had no idea what that would look like yet, but she was eager to find out.

Printed in Great Britain
by Amazon